WALT DISNEY
101
DALMATIANS

Hi! My name is Pongo. This story began one spring day while Roger, my pet, was trying to write a song. He was practically married to his work. I was worried we would be bachelors forever. Boring.

So I was looking out the window for a suitable mate. Two really — one for me and one for Roger.

That's when I saw her — a beautiful Dalmatian. Her human looked nice, too. "Perfect!" I decided.

It took some quick thinking to get Roger away from his work. But soon, I was able to convince him to go for a walk.

I spotted them as soon as we entered the park, and soon managed to get their attention. The Dalmatian was named Perdita. She was wonderful.

But as usual, Roger had his head in the clouds. He barely noticed Perdita's human, Anita. Finally, I wound my leash around their legs. That got them to notice each other, all right! It also got Perdita to notice me.

Before long, Roger asked Anita to marry him, and Perdita agreed to marry me, too. It was a beautiful double wedding.

We were all excited when we discovered that Perdita was going to have puppies. When I finally saw them, all fifteen, I was the proudest father on the block!

Then Cruella de Vil burst through the door, and shattered our peace. "I heard that Perdita and Pongo have fifteen puppies," Cruella said, pulling out a checkbook. "How much do you want for all of them?"

When Anita and Roger explained that the puppies were not for sale, Cruella stormed out of the house, shouting threats. I had the feeling she meant trouble.

Over the next few weeks, the puppies grew quickly. They were such fun! Their hero was a television star named Thunderbolt.

Then, one night, Perdita and I went out for our walk with Roger and Anita, and left the puppies at home with Nanny.

As soon as we had left, two men came to the door, pretending they worked for the electric company. Nanny wouldn't let them in, but they pushed their way past her. Soon, they found what they were after – the puppies! Nanny tried her best, but she couldn't stop them.

When we got home, we found the puppies' basket empty.

Roger called the police right away. But Perdita and I decided we had to do something, too. So I used the Twilight Bark to send out word of the kidnapping. Soon all of the dogs in London were barking the news. What a racket! But it worked.

After a while, a Great Dane barked the message to Towser the bloodhound and Lucy the goose. They passed it on to the Colonel, an old English sheepdog who lived out in the countryside.

"It's a kidnapping. Puppies . . . fifteen Dalmatian puppies . . . last night," the Colonel told his friend Tibs the cat.

"I just remembered," said Tibs. "Two nights past, I heard puppies barking at the old de Vil mansion."

"That place has been empty for years. Something fishy is going on over there," the Colonel said. "Let's go have a look."

Sure enough, there were signs of activity at the old mansion.

The Colonel sent Tibs to get a closer look.

What a scene! Two tough-looking men named Horace and Jasper were watching television. And all around them were spotted puppies! Tibs snuck closer to one of the puppies.

"Are you one of the fifteen stolen puppies?" Tibs whispered.

"There's ninety-nine of us altogether," answered the pup.

Tibs knew there was no time to waste when he overheard Cruella de Vil arrive at the house and begin talking to Horace and Jasper. She was planning to make spotted coats out of the puppies!

"Quick!" Tibs whispered to the puppies. "Follow me and don't make a sound! You're in danger. I've got to get you out of here now!"

Tibs led the puppies to a hole in the living room wall. Then, just as he was pushing the last one through, Horace and Jasper noticed the dogs were missing.

Jasper grabbed a fireplace poker, and Horace picked up a broken chair leg to use as a club. Then they started searching every corner of the old mansion.

Quickly, Tibs hid the puppies under the staircase. "Shush!" the cat whispered. But just then, the flashlight's beam lit up their hiding place!

Meanwhile Perdita and I had received word that the puppies had been found. We burst into the mansion just in time.

I latched onto Jasper's leg and soon had him on the floor. Meanwhile, Perdita made short work of Horace.

Then Perdita and I and all the puppies ran safely to a barn, where we planned to hide out for a while. But when Horace and Jasper showed up there, we all had to move on.

The weather was getting worse, and it was hard for the puppies to walk in the deep snow. I had to carry one of the pups.

Finally, a collie came out to meet us. "We have shelter for you at the dairy farm across the road. You can all rest and get an early start in the morning."

"Thank goodness!" I said.

The next day at dawn, we were on the run again. A Labrador retriever was waiting for us at the next village. He gave us shelter and explained that he had arranged a ride home for us in the back of a truck.

Just then, Cruella de Vil roared into the village in her car, followed by Horace and Jasper in their truck.

"Oh, Pongo," said Perdita, spotting Cruella through the window of the shop where we were hiding. "How will we get into the truck without her seeing us?"

Then I had an idea. "We'll all roll in soot," I said. "She's looking for dogs with spots, not black dogs."

Soon we were all black from head to tail. Then Perdita and the Lab led a batch of puppies right past Horace and Jasper, and into the waiting truck.

"Wouldn't it be funny if the Dalmatians disguised themselves?" Horace remarked as the puppies trotted past him.

"You idiot!" Jasper laughed. "Dogs don't paint themselves black!"

"Those dogs are somewhere in this village!" Cruella yelled to Horace and Jasper. "Now, go find them!"

The final batch of puppies had almost made it to the truck when . . .

SPLAAT! A drop of melting snow fell on one of the puppies.

In an instant, Cruella recognized the puppies. "After them! After them!" she cried.

ust as I lifted the last puppy safely into the truck, he engine roared to life, and we were all on our vay to London.

I'll catch up with hem yet!" Cruella said, s she drove after us.

Cruella raced after the truck, trying to force it off the road.

Just when it looked as if she were going to catch up to us, Horace and Jasper's truck came barrelling down the hill from another direction, and smashed into Cruella's car. BAANNG! CRAASSHH! Cruella, Horace and Jasper went flying through the air and landed in a pile of snow.

A little later, at the house in London, Nanny heard barking. Then the kitchen door burst open, and a pack of black dogs scampered in. One of the big dogs jumped on Anita's lap. "It's Perdy!" she cried.

"And all the puppies!" Anita said as Nanny dusted the coal dust off them. Then she looked again. "There must be a hundred of them!" she said in amazement.

"One hundred and one," said Roger, counting.

"What will we do with them all?" asked Anita.

"We'll keep 'em," said Roger. "We'll buy a big place in the country and live there. It'll be a plantation. A Dalmatian plantation!"

Good old Roger. That's exactly what he did.